Otto

HE BOOK BEAR

For my mother

OTTO THE BOOK BEAR

A JONATHAN CAPE BOOK
978 1 780 08003 1

Published in Great Britain by Jonathan Cape,
an imprint of Random House Children's Books
A Random House Group Company
This edition published 2011
3 5 7 9 10 8 6 4 2
Copyright © Katie Cleminson, 2011

The right of Katie Cleminson to be identified
as the author and illustrator of this work has
been asserted in accordance with the Copyright,
Designs and Patents Act 1988.
All rights reserved.

RANDOM HOUSE CHILDREN'S BOOKS
61–63 Uxbridge Road, London W5 5SA

www.kidsatrandomhouse.co.uk

JONATHAN
CAPE
LIBRARY

Addresses for companies within The Random House
Group Limited can be found at:
www.randomhouse.co.uk/offices.htm
THE RANDOM HOUSE GROUP
Limited Reg. No. 954009
A CIP catalogue record for this book is
available from the British Library.

Printed and bound in China

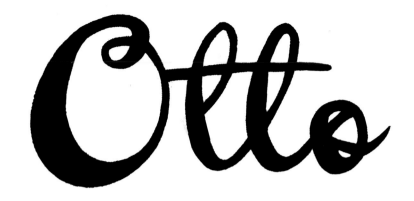

Otto

THE BOOK BEAR

KATIE CLEMINSON

Jonathan Cape
London

Once upon a time…

Otto was a book bear.

He lived in a book on a shelf in a house . . .

and he was at his happiest when
children read his book.

But Otto also had a special secret.

When no one was looking,

he came to life!

Once upon a time...

Otto loved to
explore the
house,

to read his favourite stories and
practise his writing.

But one day something terrible happened . . .

and Otto was left behind.

Otto didn't like being all alone.
So he made a plan, packed a bag

and set off on a
new adventure.

But the world outside made
Otto feel very small.

Nobody seemed to notice him.

Otto began to search the city, hoping to find a new place to live. But nowhere he went felt like home.

It was too busy, too wet, too cold, too smokey,

too high, too windy

and too unwelcoming.

Otto didn't like living in the city,
and he missed his warm book.

He was starting to feel downhearted. But he decided to pick up his bag and carry on walking.

And just when
he thought he
couldn't walk
any further,
when he felt
cold and tired,

Otto saw a place that
looked full of light
and hope.

He went inside and found . . .

. . . rows and rows of **books!**

Otto began
to climb,

and there, at the end of the shelf,
he saw something.

Could it be . . .?

It was!

Another book bear!

The other bear shook Otto's paw
and said, "I'm Ernest.
How do you do?"

Otto's new friend showed him around the library

and he discovered it was full of book creatures
just like him.

Together with Ernest,
he could once again
read his favourite
stories,

This morning we looked
through maps and a book
about a brave ?dition
to Mount ?

practise his
writing

and try out all
kinds of exciting
new things.

LOANED

LOANED

And the best part was . . .

now Otto had
lots of readers –
and that made
him the happiest
book bear of all.

...happily ever after.